The Sailboat and the Sea:

ENCOUNTERS WITH GOD THROUGH THE JOURNEY OF LIFE

Endorsements

I read a lot—not because I have to, but because I love to. And I absolutely love this book. Many people tend to write to show what they know and how much you don't know. But from page one I knew this was going to be a truly unique experience.

The Sailboat and the Sea is packed cover to cover with wisdom, but not the "I'm smarter than you" kind—more of a childlike wisdom. Anyone can understand what's being taught. Literally even a child could read this and "get it."

And that's the best kind of writing. I highly recommend this creative take on the relationship between you and your Creator.

    —**Robert Cook**, Pastor, Author, Speaker and Disciple of my Lord and Savior

Brilliantly written. Powerful. Relevant. Engaging. *The Sailboat and the Sea* skillfully represents two sides of God's immense capacity to shepherd us within his paternal and maternal characteristics. He meets us as a father: a protector, a disciplinarian. Then as a mother pouring out unconditional love, a gentle nurturer. When we can consciously draw upon the fullness of God as both father and mother, it is then that we become keenly aware of our completeness in him. In this delightful book, Peter Lundell captures the relentless human struggle during tumultuous storms, and illustrates the mighty yet loving heart of God that provides all of our needs. I saw myself throughout this endearing work.

    —**Carol L. Brooks**, Author, *Uncharted Territory*

In trying to explain *The Sailboat and the Sea* to myself, I settled on *allegory*, although it can also be a book of tender devotional reads. It fits into the same category as Hannah Hurnard's story about Much Afraid in *Hinds'*

Feet on High Places. Or Christian in John Bunyan's 400-year-old classic, *Pilgrim's Progress*.

The book is a dialog between LittleBoat talking to BigSea about the problems of life. The warm tones and obvious compassion shine through in such a way that readers readily realize *they are the little boat*.

—**Cecil Murphey**, author or co-author of more than a hundred books, several of which have appeared on the New York Times bestseller list. His titles include *90 Minutes in Heaven*, co-written with Don Piper and *Gifted Hands: The Ben Carson Story*.

This wonderfully creative and unique devotional book will deepen your relationship with the Lord. Each short chapter provides much Truth to ponder. Like LittleBoat you'll find yourself engaging in conversations with the Lord that will change your life. Highly recommended!

—**Marlene Bagnull**, Author, Speaker & Director of Write His Answer Ministries

Reading *The Sailboat and the Sea* has confirmed for me what I've always suspected: Peter Lundell is a Christian mystic. There is simply no other word that is apt to explain his uncanny connection between humanness and spirituality. With his masterful use of language, Peter forms a wonderful bridge helping us to move with effortlessly between those two worlds.

—**Michael Gantt**, Speaker, Missionary, Author, *Sharpening the Iron of the Church*

A practical self-examination, using an easy to understand and comprehend conversational format. This book challenges us to ask and review the tough questions and what might be our priorities as we move into the unknown future.

—**Chuck Fountain**, Louisiana District Superintendent, Church of the Nazarene

The Sailboat and the Sea:

ENCOUNTERS WITH GOD THROUGH THE JOURNEY OF LIFE

Peter Lundell

*A sailboat encounters the sea for a
heart-and-mind-swirling journey with God.*

Copyright Notice

The Sailboat and the Sea: Encounters with God through the Journey of Life

First edition. Copyright © 2019 by Peter Lundell. The information contained in this book is the intellectual property of Peter Lundell and is governed by United States and International copyright laws. All rights reserved. No part of this publication, either text or image, may be used for any purpose other than personal use. Therefore, reproduction, modification, storage in a retrieval system, or retransmission, in any form or by any means, electronic, mechanical, or otherwise, for reasons other than personal use, except for brief quotations for reviews or articles and promotions, is strictly prohibited without prior written permission by the publisher.

Cover and Interior Design: Derinda Babcock

Editor(s): Susan K. Stewart, Deb Haggerty

Author Represented by Credo Communications

PUBLISHED BY: Elk Lake Publishing, Inc., 35 Dogwood Dr., Plymouth, MA 02360, 2019

Library Cataloging Data

Names: Lundell, Peter (Peter Lundell)

The Sailboat and the Sea: Encounters with God through the Journey of Life / Peter Lundell

130p. 23cm × 15cm (9in × 6 in.)

Description: A sailboat encounters the sea for a heart-and-mind-swirling journey with God.

Identifiers: ISBN-13: 978-1-948888-83-7 (trade) | 978-1-948888-84-4 (POD) | 978-1-948888-85-1 (e-book.)

Key Words: sailing, inspirational, life, discovery, spiritual knowledge, self-discovery, devotional

LCCN: 2018961532 Fiction

Dedication

To Drs. Dan and MaryAnn Nusbaum,
who invited me to sail with them
across the middle of the Pacific Ocean
on their sailing vessel StarReach.
On that sailing trip
the ideas for this book were born.
Thank you, thank you, thank you.

Table of Contents

Beginnings
    1. Who Are You?....................1
    2. Who Am I?......................5
    3. Look What I Have 9
    4. Life Stinks....................13
    5. I Was Abused 17
    6. I Feel Rejected................21
    7. I'm Afraid 25

Awakenings
    8. Been There and Done That 29
    9. I Messed up. Is There Hope? 35
    10. Can I Trust You?..............39
    11. What Is the Truth? 43
    12. What Is Love?.................47
    13. I Wonder.....................51
    14. I Want to Reach the Moon 55

Struggles
    15. Where Am I Going? 61
    16. I Wish.......................65
    17. I'm a Failure 69
    18. I Hurt.......................73
    19. I'm Stressed Out 77
    20. I'm Angry....................81
    21. I'm Lost in the Storm 85

Completions
    22. I'm Worn Out..................91
    23. This Is Not What I Expected....95
    24. I'm Lonely...................99
    25. What Is My Life Worth? 103
    26. Where Does It End? 107
    27. The Enveloping Sea...........111
    28. Your Chapter.................115

About the Author 117

Beginnings

Chapter 1. Who Are You?

LittleBoat watched another sailboat slowly sink in the murky harbor water. Stern first, the mast followed like an arm reaching for help, and finally the bow slipped under water. LittleBoat shuddered. He had to get out of the harbor, away from the other boats who collected barnacles while they yakked about past voyages.

That could have been me. Or it could be me tomorrow. I'd better get sailing.
You have the present, right here, right now.
Something has to change. But I don't even know where to start.
Change is good. Look and you shall find.
Maybe there's more out there—or at least more to sailing—than I thought.
Much more.
I need to be alone and think.
But you are not alone.
I am too.
You are talking to yourself then?
No ... I must be hearing things.
You took years to hear me, but congratulations.
What? Who are you?
Just that. I am.
Where are you?
All around.
But no one's here.
Wherever I go, I am already there.
That's crazy.

The Sailboat and the Sea

Yes. To a boat.
You're freaking me out. Who are you?
Call me BigSea. I am the spirit of the sea, the creator of the sea. And more.
You never talked to me before.
You did not have ears to hear.
How do I know who you really are?
You will hear me, though not with your ears. You will see me, though not with your eyes. You will feel my presence as you ride upon my waters.
I'm supposed to believe this?
As you travel, you will choose whether you believe or not. I do not promise a nice trip. Along your journey I will allow trouble.
I don't like trouble.
Your troubled heart is what just opened your ears to me. How else will you stay close to me?
I don't want to get close to you.
You will.
Oh? And if I do, I'll just stay close without the trouble.
Not likely.
I've got my own life, so let's leave it at that.
You will love me. You will hate me. You will think I have forgotten you. You may question if I exist, because I am quiet.
This doesn't look like a happy trip.
Do not worry, LittleBoat.
How do you know my name?
I know every boat's name. And every boat's heart.
I don't even know you.
I see your love, your hate, your joy, your sadness. Whatever I see, I promise you my presence.
You'll go with me?
I am already with you—where you were, where you are, where you will be.
You're everywhere?
All the time.
Oh, really? I never saw you with me in bad times.
You only looked at your wounds.
Well, I don't see you now either.
Your eyes must learn.

Peter Lundell

Does it matter how I feel?
When your heart is grieved, LittleBoat, what will you do?
I ... I don't know.
Call to me. Even when you rage against me, call to me.
You won't reject me?
I will comfort you.
No way.
Yes.
Hmmm. I'll think about it. If I get around to it, I might even try.
Do not try. Simply do.
So it's easy?
At times the storm waves will be too much for you. Call upon me. When the waves calm and the sun shines, do not forget me.
And you'll come?
I will already be there.
So you're more than just a guide, huh?
I am the origin and substance of all being. I am your judge who rules with mercy. I am your redeemer. Your friend. I simply am.
You can't be all that.
Do not recreate me in your own image. I am not a boat. But I know your needs.
I've got lots of needs.
You will come to know me well.

Chapter 2. Who Am I?

LittleBoat unfurled his jib and thirty-foot mainsail. Through the reach of a concrete jetty, he leaned into the open sea, and the waves received him. He glanced back at the harbor as a brisk wind filled his sails. Most boats sailed close to shore. He gazed beyond his bow and his stern then into his hull.

I'm going to sail far away.
You cannot run from who you are inside.
You again?
I never left.
Leave me alone.
I am all around you.
Just don't talk to me.
But for the first time you are listening.
Because I can't get that sinking boat out of my mind.
Good.
Good? That's not good. Seeing that made me wonder why I even float in the first place.
Very good. That is why you and I are talking.
I don't want to talk, and if you knew me, you wouldn't like me.
Know me, and you will find freedom from who you are.
You wouldn't want to know who I am.
I already know.
And I suppose you love me and care about me.
More than you know.

The Sailboat and the Sea

ou really think I'll believe you love me? I'm not even worth liking.
You have not learned how I love.
So what?
But you will.
Yeah, well I'll just try to love myself if you don't mind.
Loving yourself is meaningless. Upon the waves you are almost nothing.
Oh, that's nice. You're as cruel as any big boat.
You are a speck on the sea. You live. You die. And the sea continues as before you existed.
I already feel bad. Thanks for making me feel worse.
Do you think you are worth something?
I ... I want to be worth something.
All boats do. But even if you grew powerful and well known by other boats, you cannot rightly claim significance as you sail on the sea. The sea is vast, eternal.
Yet we boats try to leave our mark.
They are scratches on the waves.
So, I'm insignificant.
On the surface.
You said I was a speck.
Go beneath the surface.
Where?
A pearl in an oyster is insignificant. But people search tirelessly for one. Though on the sea you are barely visible, in my heart you are a pearl. You are everything to me. I made the sea and all that is in it for you to sail on.
As if I'll believe that.
Seemingly nothing, but in truth, everything.
How can I be everything to you? I'm just a boat.
As you sail with me, you will learn how I love you, and as you do, your own heart will grow.
But I'm small, and no one cares who I am.
You need not be known. I know you. Though your sail may be small, travel the course I give you. You will find purpose in me. And you will live larger than yourself.
I don't even know why I'm here. What's the point of being a sailboat?
Though you did not know it, I created you, LittleBoat.
I was built in a boat yard.
Yes, you were. But everything rises from me. I designed you to be

Peter Lundell

LittleBoat. As you were constructed, you slowly took shape, first a frame, then your hull, your deck, your mast, and finally your sails. Then you learned to sail.
I've been trying a long time to sail straight.
And I have sighed with every wrong direction. You have hurt yourself many times. And I have hurt, because I carry you in my heart.
Spare me the sentiment. What do you expect of me?
Your part is to become what I've put inside you. Will you become what you were created to be?
I don't know what you're talking about.
Follow me.
Where are you—no, you're already there, right?
You are learning.
Do I need to go to some kind of boat school for this?
Only follow.
That might be harder than going to school.
Your heart grows by intention. Not every boat makes the effort to sail well. Some rarely leave the harbor.
All I needed to do in the harbor was float.
Comfort leads to rot. Pursue what you were created to be.
Let me guess. Following you won't be easy.
The effort will cost more than most are willing to pay.
Is following you worth the price?
Keep sailing, LittleBoat. And you will learn the answer.

Chapter 3. Look What I Have

Sunlight sparkled in the water and fractured across the surface like a million pieces of crystal. LittleBoat thought he'd impress the other boats by polishing and displaying his gadgets.

BigSea, let me show you all my stuff.
Impress me.
I met a boat with things to sell, and I couldn't help but buy more.
And now you feel better.
Yes. Look at my new compass! It's made of brass, with oversized numbers on a liquid base, and it's gimbaled, so that however I tip, the compass will always be level. See?
How nice.
And my winches are new and expensive. They have two torques. Clockwise, one turn per two inches of line; counter-clockwise, one turn per four inches. See how shiny they are?
Astonishing.
You're not really impressed.
You are boasting of toys.
But I'm not a big boat, and I sail as well as any other. I deserve something to show off.
You deserve something. Really?
I do. What would other boats think of me otherwise?
Do you care what they think? You do not even like them.
Like them or not, impressions are important.
To a fool—who thinks he owns his toys when his toys in fact own him.

The Sailboat and the Sea

Oh, that's like a torpedo below the waterline. These things are all I have to be proud of—and they're expensive.
That is even worse.
No, it's better.
You could have shared with lesser boats. That would have been better.
Not to me. I like my stuff.
Are you so proud of what you own?
Most boats are.
Most boats ignore me.
But I thought they knew you.
They disregard what they know and sail their own courses.
And you don't like all my stuff. Do you want me to be impoverished?
I want to bless you.
Then why are you so unimpressed with what I have?
Your gadgets distract you and keep you busy tending them rather than truly sailing.
But with them I can do so much.
As you pay more attention to your things, you pay less attention to me.
Well, my things need attention.
That is my point.
Shouldn't I take good care of my things?
Certainly. But be aware possessions can dominate your thoughts and concerns until they even hijack your heart.
I don't think so. I'm in control.
Perhaps on the surface. Deeper down your possessions can give you a false sense of independence and lead you to think you do not need me.
Many boats dream of that.
As you think you are independent, you turn your stern at me.
But I love my cool stuff.
Be careful of what you love.
Are possessions really so bad?
No, they are not. But too many of them or too much love for them is a symptom.
Of what?
Pride. The kind that covers an empty heart and lack of meaning.
Do I want to hear this?
They reveal the centrality of self and the myth of one's importance at the core of everything that defies me.
The old ego thing, eh?

Eternally so.
So what's your suggestion?
The way up is down and the way down is up.
Which means?
Exalt yourself and I will humble you. Humble yourself and I will exalt you.
That's a lot of letting go.
Who keeps you afloat? Who blows your sails?
We both know the answer.
I could swamp you with one wave.
Ahh—I get the picture.
Some boats define themselves by their impressive design and beauty of their sails.
I could use a new sail.
They hoard wealth, try to impress, and are themselves impressed by the superficial glitz that most boats call reality.
You must admit, they are impressive.
In the eyes of a boat. But they are hollow inside. And when they sink, there remains only an empty hull.
Um, can we talk about the weather?
I am not impressed with what you have, LittleBoat. Those things are nothing to me. Your desire for toys crowds my presence from your heart.
As I think about it, I do feel some hollow spots.
I can fill them better than any gadget.
I'd like that, but is there no way to impress you?
By the journey you sail.

Chapter 4. Life Stinks

The afternoon sun cast a blinding swath across the sea's expanse. A yacht came toward LittleBoat, and though they were the only two boats in sight, the bigger boat turned straight toward LittleBoat, then veered away, leaving him to thrash in its wake.

BigSea, I hate boats like that. I hate that I can't do anything about them.
Their actions are regrettable, but so is your perception.
It's not fair that I'm so small and others are so big. Life stinks!
Of course life is not fair. But is it fair that you are a boat while some are makeshift rafts?
I didn't want to go that far.
Yet I must. I watch over all that floats.
Well, they're just rafts.
And is it fair that some boats are permanently damaged while you are not?
That's not my fault.
Nor is it fair. If your journey were fair, you would sink right now.
Now that I think about it, that might not be such a bad idea.
I will not allow it.
Why not?
Your voyage is not yet over.
What gives you the right to tell me my life's itinerary?
I am the Sea.
So?
I shall sink you right now then. Pardon me while I churn up a whirlpool.
No, no, no. Ah ... let's, ummm ... start over.

The Sailboat and the Sea

I am the Sea.
Got it. And I'm a boat.
You are unhappy with your voyage.
That's right. What are you going to do about it?
Nothing.
Nothing?
Your happiness is not my concern. Your nearness to me concerns me greatly.
You don't care about my happiness?
Happiness is superficial. Connecting with me brings you life, which brings you joy, no matter what the nature of your voyage may be.
I'll keep that in mind … Will my voyage get better?
You are still more concerned about being happy.
But will my voyage get better?
You hold the answer. Rather than lamenting, speak of what you will do with who you are.
Should I know what you're talking about?
Accept what you cannot change.
That's a lot of things.
Change what you can.
Not many of them.
More than you think.
What do you expect from me?
That which you are able to give.
It's not much.
Far more than you admit.
How would you know?
You do not know how much you can give until you have given everything you can. Then you will begin to know what you can give.
Sailing with you is scary.
And sailing without me is dangerous.
Just once, I'd like an easy choice.
Important choices are rarely easy. But despite circumstances you choose your attitude.
I hate big boats. They control and abuse small boats.
Do not let them control your heart.
And big boats get whatever they want.
But they are imprisoned by who they become.
They take all kinds of advantages and even break the law.

Take heart. The more they break, the less they can escape. I am the ultimate law. And they all collide with me eventually, whether while they float or after they sink.
I'll bet that's not pretty.
It is not. But I grieve each time.
You're sad even though they break the law and sink?
Justice punishes. Love hurts.
I hope you're nice to me when my time comes.
That is up to you.
It's my choice? I thought you had my journey planned.
Both are true.
How can they be? They're contradictory.
I am beyond your reason.
Fine.
And far beyond your selfishness.
My selfishness?
You lament only for yourself. You complain about others, and you protest your voyage.
You're going to tell me about the broken-down rafts again, aren't you?
You will find me closer to them, and boats who care for them, than to any others. Because those who suffer find their home in me, which is how they endure.
So if I want to be close to you ...
You must be close to those who suffer.
Then I might suffer too.
That is the idea.

Chapter 5. I Was Abused

Lights on shore twinkled in the twilight. Along the coast they spread like a hundred winking eyes, each concealing a secret. LittleBoat carried secrets too, secrets that hurt, memories that refused to sleep, wounds that others had inflicted and would not confess.

BigSea, I was abused.
I know.
I'm dirty inside.
I will not reject you.
Violated, my innocence stolen.
Because you are mine, I was violated too.
Why didn't you do anything? How could you have let those things happen to me?
For the same reason I give you freedom to think and do bad things.
I don't know if I want to hear this.
Any meaningful relationship I have with boats requires freedom. I am sorry for some of the inevitable consequences.
Freedom is painful. Sometimes I hate it.
I understand.
There must be a less painful way to run the world.
There is. You could be a machine.
Make me a machine.
I love you too much to do that. The mindlessness of mechanical existence is a dull horror.
I don't believe you.
You have never been a machine.

The Sailboat and the Sea

Those who committed the crime and escaped capture from other boats will not escape me.
If you're so big, why don't you do something to them now? Hit them hard. Sink them!
They will meet their opportunity to repent, and they will meet their fate, whether by the law, by their own demise, or by me.
But you don't know what it's like to be abused.
Actually, I do.
How could you be abused?
You would be surprised.
My whole world seems dark. Do you know how that feels?
Oh, yes. When you are mistreated, I feel with you. I absorb your hurt as you give it to me.
And what do you do with the pain?
Shared pain leads to shared life.
My hull has permanent dents.
I was there. I felt the beating.
That's hard to believe.
My waters surround you. How could I not feel it?
You didn't do anything to stop them.
You said freedom was painful. That is the price of not being a machine.
I don't get it.
Would you rather I intervene in every mishap, every misfortune, even before it happens?
That would be nice.
Would it? Whether a mishap is yours or someone else's, every boat would eventually grow completely careless and irresponsible. Would they not?
Because they would always expect you to bail them out.
And boats would sail recklessly and inflict themselves on others to the point of insanity. Life would become intolerable.
Do we have to think that far ahead?
I am already there.
Well, at least in this lifetime, I'd like to be a healed, happy boat.
Give your pain to me. I will give back healing.
Even if my hull heals, my heart feels as if it's been stabbed and the knife left there.
And the pain doesn't go away.

Peter Lundell

The blade cuts the wound over and over so it never heals.
My heart was stabbed along with yours.
My heart is still bleeding.
I bled too. Grow close to me. The way you see your pain will change, and you will let the agony go.
Get real. How can I let it go?
You must decide to recover.
I don't want to.
Then suffer. You have made your choice, and I will not change it for you.
Don't you understand? Someone cut me open and gouged out my guts!
And when you stuff them back inside, they do not fit right. They never feel the same, ever.

~ ~ ~ ~

Keep sailing with me, LittleBoat. Together we will realign your cargo.
I'd rather be bitter.
I love you too much to let you keep yourself bound in pain.
How will sailing with you make anything different?
You will let your bitterness go, and you will be free. Then you will once again grow close to others.
I can't trust anyone enough to get close. I won't.
How painful will your freedom become?
I want to feel better.
Then choose. Sail with me and be restored. From there you can get close to others.
I'll bet you have this whole thing already mapped out.
I do. But you still must choose.
You'd make life a lot easier if you didn't let bad things happen in the first place.
Letting bad things happen is the hardest part.
Yes, for me.
And for me.

Chapter 6. I Feel Rejected

LittleBoat trimmed his sail to a broad reach and continued toward blue water. He slid down the rocking troughs and splashed through the slapping waves. Off his starboard bow drifted a wooden raft, bare and lifeless, bobbing one way, then another. A memory returned to LittleBoat.

I sometimes feel like that raft … shoved out to sea to drift all alone.
I carry more neglected rafts than you could know.
Some boats treat me as if no matter what I do, I'm wrong—
They inflict the fantasy of their pride on anyone in their path.
—or I'm never good enough.
They will not cease until their curses turn and claw at their own soul.
I didn't do anything wrong.
Be careful LittleBoat, no boat can be completely right—
Well, I feel cast out.
—especially those boats who continually think they are right.
Other boats have shoved me off, turned their sterns on me, and sailed away.
I feel how much your rejection hurts. I have seen many boat sterns.
How can you feel that? I thought you were all around.
There are boats who disdain me. They wish me to be like one of them.
    But even if I were, they would spurn me still more.
How can they do that? You are the sea!
The hearts of some boats can be like dark water and hide both good and bad.
I think they hide mostly bad.
Some do, but not all.

The Sailboat and the Sea

The bad is what we feel the most.
And the deepest.
They can sink for all I care.
Now you are rejecting them—and becoming like them.
Why can't I get back at them?
Because when you do, you mostly hurt yourself.
I don't want to hear that.
I know.
Just make me happy.
Only you can do that. Regardless of what I do, happiness is your own choice. But happiness is secondary. Better to seek joy, also a choice, and its source runs deep.
Yeah, whatever.
LittleBoat, you are shivering.
No, I'm not.
The water is vibrating all around your hull.
Okay, okay. I feel lonely and cold. The whole world feels cold, and there's no place to warm up.
Rejection is cold, no matter where you go. To warm up, you must find acceptance.
Let me guess, that comes from you too, right?
Do you believe that?
I want to be loved. And to love. I reach out, but every embrace feels empty.
Let my waters enfold you.
But I don't ...
Will you continue to indulge yourself with whining, or will you look to me?
Why do I have to choose?
Life is choices, even if I am in control.
I hate everyone who ever rejected me. They can all sink.
LittleBoat, you will cause yourself to sink even before they do.
I don't care.
I think you do.
Okay, what if I do?
Receive my embrace. Let your rejection flow into me and let my acceptance flow into you.
It's hard.
Which is why so few boats do it.

~~~~

Peter Lundell

Are you feeling better?
Yes. And warm.
Now that you feel better, what will you do?
Just be happy.
More than that, LittleBoat. Will you still reject other boats, even if they reject you?
I didn't think about that.
Because you only thought of yourself. Can you forgive those who reject you?
How can I? They despise me. I still think they deserve to sink.
So do you.
Why do you have to bring that up?
Because of my love and mercy, you still float.
But what about them?
They are not your concern. They will come to me, or not come, on their own.
What about all they did to me?
The more you harbor self-pity, the more corrupt your own heart becomes.
You talk as if what they did is my problem.
Ultimately it *is* your problem because it is your heart. So release your self-pity, just as you release your pain and anger.
It's hard to let go. I'm so used to them.
I will help you, and you can receive my acceptance in return. Did I not already absorb your rejection in my embrace? Did I not accept you?
You did.
Forgive them despite what they say or do. Forgive them because of who you are.
Even if they continue to scorn me?
You will have me.

Chapter 7. I'm Afraid

The wind increased and whistled between the halyards and sails. Waves jostled and crested in whitecaps stark against the darkening sky and darkening water.

BigSea! Your waves are too rough. They're beating against me. They'll swallow me!
Waves are the nature of the sea, LittleBoat. They are the nature of life. Sometimes they are gentle, sometimes rough.
But you're the sea!
And the spirit of the sea.
Can't you tell the waves to calm?
I could.
Why don't you?
You would grow weak, proud, and complacent. Then you would forget me.
I wouldn't forget you, BigSea.
Boats without affliction often do.
Isn't there an easier way?
You would not like that course.
Where does it go?
Forward for a while, then in circles, then nowhere. Too many boats go in circles, while telling themselves they're on a journey. Some boats go nowhere at all. Did you not see them in the harbor?
Moored to the docks, barnacles covering their hulls.
They exist, but they do not live. I made you for a journey, LittleBoat.
That's nice, but why does mine have to be so hard?
So your life has meaning.

The Sailboat and the Sea

I'm tired of meaning.
The lack of it is worse.
Argh! Do I have to go through this?
If you want to truly live.
Sometimes I just wish—
Do not waste attention wishing. Overcome.
That's easy to say.
Look at the waves again.
They're still big. Bigger than I am.
Are they bigger than I am?
No, BigSea. Of course you're bigger.
Then ride them, LittleBoat. Ride through them. Over them. Around them. You will pitch and rock, but you will not sink. I will hold you from beneath.
I'll try, BigSea.
When you are with me, nothing is bigger than you.
I see some monster waves.
They look small to me.
How can I see them as you do?
Do not see them from behind; they will never stop chasing. Do not see them from the side; they will always crash upon you. Face forward and throw your fear into them. Then break through their beating.
That's crazy.
Going forward is the way of those who break through waves.
I don't know about this.
Knowing will come as you do it.
On the other side is just more water.
On the other side is your future.
What is my future?
You must open it.
Don't I even get a hint?
Your future is intertwined with me.
Like everything else.
Yes, for those who pay attention.
I'm still afraid. The monster waves are getting closer.
I am with you in the waves. And in the water beyond the waves.
Will I make it?
That is the wrong question.
What then?

Peter Lundell

Ask yourself if you are with me.
But you're everywhere.
What does that matter to you?
What should I ask?
Am I in your heart? Do you trust me?
Yes, I think ... Oh no!
The waves are rising, LittleBoat.
You were right about trouble drawing me closer to you.
It is the way of every journey.
The waves are like mountains!
Go, LittleBoat, and hold your rudder firm.
Here goes.
Always face forward.
What if—
Trust.
Hold me, BigSea. Don't let me go.
I am. Are you holding on to me?

Awakenings

Chapter 8. Been There, Done That

From a hazy sky, a breeze splashed water onto the foredeck. A flying fish leaped out of the waves and flapped its fins across the bow. But LittleBoat had seen many flying fish before.

BigSea, everywhere I go I feel that I've been there, done that.
Did you forget how scared you were of the big waves? And how you overcame them?
I'm proud that with you I overcame them. But since then I've gotten bored with the waves, the whitecaps, the wind in my sails, the cloud formations, even the sunsets. All I see is liquid real estate that turns hills into valleys that turn back into hills.
I do not exist to entertain you.
I'm bored with sailing.
You have misplaced your wonder.
That's just for baby boats.
And older boats who remember how to live.
Well, I'm busy sailing.
And you see only yourself. You care little for others or for my creation.
I can't always think about other boats or your creation.
It is part of every boat's purpose.
Why do you tell me all this serious stuff?
Because you will never leave the sea alive.
So what do I do? Sink?
Yes. But before you do, sail differently. Sail meaningfully, as you said you would.
I can't seem to do that very well.

The Sailboat and the Sea

So much lies around you that you have not seen.
I've seen everything a gazillion times.
You have barely begun to see.
What more is there besides sightseeing in a new location?
When you open your eyes, do you see, or do you merely look?
Aren't they the same?
They are as different as waking and sleeping.
Sometimes I'd rather sleep.
When you hear, do you listen?
I hadn't thought about it.
An ear can choose to be numb, or to be aware.
What if I don't respond?
You will grow callous until you cannot hear.
And end up in trouble, I suppose.
And you'll groan and ask why I let it happen.
You heard me groaning last time, didn't you?
As you sail, do you feel my presence, or do you only move?
I guess the journey is more than just going to my destination.
You have not fully lived, LittleBoat. You have merely existed.
Do we need to have this conversation?
You started it because deep inside you know. Your heart longs to be
 fully alive.
How do you know that?
Were you happy in the harbor?
No, I just listened to other blowhards yak about their past.
So you left that to sail again, to do what you were created to do.
That's a good way to put it.
Thus you desire to know me, and to live, more than you admit.
Okay, I give in. Teach me to live.
That is why I am with you.
What should I do?
Read my waves. In them you will see me. As you see me, you will see
 yourself in me.
I'm looking.
See. Hear. Feel. All will become different—each ray of sun that penetrates
 the surface, the birds that fly above, the fish that swim beneath.
They've always done that.
But you have not paid them any attention. Thus you have deprived
 yourself.

What do I have to do, follow them around?
Silly boat. Watch them, hear them, feel them.
I get the sense that's more than just being entertained.
Be entertained if you like. But beware of dulling your mind to the reality around you. My creation bears my imprint at every point.
How will I know if I dull my mind?
You will be bored.
As I am now.
Yes, LittleBoat. Wake up.
Will it really be different?
The sea is full of wonder if you have the will to see.
I'm wondering what more there is to notice.
A world's worth. You have not found your part in the mosaic of life. All is connected. And all connects to me.
Sounds philosophical.
No, merely a simple choice of seeing beyond yourself and how you fit in my big picture.
So what do you suggest?
When you love me, you will love others.
What do others have to do with all this?
Engaging your journey with that of others grows the meaning and purpose of your journey itself.
Will I stop being bored?
Life will awaken within you.

Chapter 9. I Messed up. Is There Hope?

Like a suspended medallion, the sun hung over a steel blue haze that appeared to fuse with the sea. To LittleBoat, the seamless horizon was like a dream.

I wish a lot of things in my past never happened. I wish they were just dreams.
Every boat does.
There were times when other boats needed my help, and I ignored them.
I found someone else to help. In your selfishness, you were the one who needed more help.
I didn't need any help.
Others needed help with their rigging and their loads. You needed help with your soul.
My soul? Is that why other boats called me a jerk?
You tell me.
Ummm. I cut them off so I could get the good wind.
And you were proud of yourself for doing it so well.
I got mad and rammed another boat. I almost sank her.
I felt the pain of that boat. We had a long talk about you.
I did things in the dark that I'd rather not talk about.
I saw them all.
Ouch ...
What will you do about all those things, LittleBoat?
Sail away.
You cannot escape that which is part of you. Your past will always follow.
I'll sail across the whole ocean.
Your darkness will meet you on the other side.

The Sailboat and the Sea

I'll ignore it.
Will that help you?
I'll just pretend everything is fine.
As most boats do.
They do?
You would be surprised at how much rot lies beneath bright paint and glistening sails.
Looking at myself, I'm not surprised.
For a long time you ignored me and pretended I did not exist.
I thought it would work.
LittleBoat, I have given myself so that your life could be redeemed.
But I'm filthy.
You are. And you smell.
Thanks a lot. Why don't you just stay away from me?
That would not be in my nature.
Okay then. Why do you even talk to me?
So I can wash you.
I'll make you dirty.
No, I will make you clean.
Why would you do that?
I desire to be near my boats. But their filth keeps me separated from them.
Must be a bummer.
I have grieved, and I have known wrath.
Are you totally pure, and you don't want to get dirty?
More than that. My nature does not mix with theirs. They must be made clean.
Do you use a scrub brush?
I wash and scatter the dirt of their hearts.
Oh, the stuff you can't see. Where do you send it?
How far is east from west?
Both are here on my compass.
How far apart are they?
They're directions. If they had distance, they'd be infinitely apart.
That is how far I will cast your wrongdoings from me.
But I deserve to sink.
I am glad you know that.
Then why don't you sink me?
Because of my love and mercy. I forgive.

Peter Lundell

Does forgiveness mean everything is all right?
No. Everything is not all right. But I release my anger against you. I absolve you from punishment. And I reconcile your separation from me.
How do you do all that?
Long ago, I, or you might say part of me, took the form of a boat and sailed. When I sank I took on myself the evil of all the other boats. I came alive again in my depths. And I want you to have that life from me.
Pretty heavy stuff.
Much better than what you're trying to do on your own.
You get me every time. So what should I do?
Confess. Empty yourself. Receive my spirit into yourself.
I can't believe you'd let me do all that.
It is my nature. When you are forgiven you—we—will make things right.
May I dump my dirty cargo overboard?
I am waiting.
Here it is. Forgive me. Save me from the results of what I've done.
~ ~ ~ ~
I am yours and you are mine.
Hold me in your waves.
Anything else?
Save me from myself.

Chapter 10. Can I Trust You?

Fog crept under darkening clouds that enveloped the sky. Reflecting the numbness above, the waters turned gray. The wind shifted then turned back again as rain began to fall. The whole world felt gray.

BigSea, I don't know what's ahead.
Do not worry about what is ahead. I am with you.
The sky is dark and rainy and cold, and so is the water.
Learn to trust me.
But I can't see anything.
Especially when you cannot see.
Can I really trust you?
Whatever I tell you will make little difference.
Tell me anyway.
Do you truly believe me?
Well, you're the sea.
That is not an answer. Belief means little unless you live what you believe.
Then I want to experience living it.
Experience is a hard teacher, LittleBoat.
I think I can handle it.
Can you handle what is coming?
BigSea, no! That wave will destroy me!
Trust.

~ ~ ~ ~

Whew! I'm still floating.
Of course you are. Most things you worry about never happen.
Worrying comes naturally to me.

The Sailboat and the Sea

And it distracts your focus and energy away from overcoming a challenge.
Can't I just run away from them?
I made you to overcome.
What if I fail?
Then fail. Failure will teach you. And you will try again.
But I could make a wrong decision.
Mistakes will teach you.
What if it they don't?
Then you are a fool.
But I want a life that works.
If you do not know me, it does not matter whether anything works.
Knowing you is hard.
Not knowing me is harder.

~~~~

I can't win with you.
Listen to me, LittleBoat. It is essential that you lose to me. Only then will you truly sail with me.
You really want me to lose?
That is the path to winning. You must give up your own course before you can sail mine.
But I feel so uncertain.
Of course you do. And in your uncertainty, look to me.
Tell me what I need to know.
Nothing. Only me.
I need a plan.
You need me.
But you said you're always with me.
Are you always with me?
I thought so.
Most boats get distracted. Remembering me is a choice.
I'll try not to forget.
Experience will stretch your ability to trust.
Then what?
Hopefully your trust will grow and keep growing.
How about we let that go for now.
Here is a bigger wave.
I don't want—
We do not always have choices.
I'm going to capsize!

Peter Lundell

Be quiet and sail.
~ ~ ~ ~
Ack! I'm ... I'm still here.
And so am I.
I think I have a lot to learn.
Some boats become battered from experience, but they do not grow wise.
    I hope your journey is different, LittleBoat.
It has to be. I can't keep sailing the way I used to.
I am glad to hear that.
Where do I start?
Right here. Always here and now.
Do you give lessons?
I have been all along.
Ah, I guess you have.
Decide now, LittleBoat. How will you sail?
Ummm ... how about with your hands beneath me?
Very good. Look closely and you will see them.

Chapter 11. What is the Truth?

The morning sun crept above the horizon to cast its rays across gentle waves. Emerald water gave way to royal blue as LittleBoat pushed farther out to sea. The waves sparkled with slivers of sun that pierced into the deep blue.

Do all the boats on these waves know you?
Some do. Many do not.
How can they not?
They assume that because they float, their voyage is satisfactory. They do not acknowledge who I am—they only enjoy my benefits.
Will they reach safe harbor?
~~~~
*Big Sea, you are silent.*
Many will not.
*Will they be lost at sea?*
Yes. And the more lost they get, the more they will think themselves wise.
*How can that be?*
They think there are many ultimate truths. Or none.
*Are there not many truths?*
There are many lesser truths.
*So each boat can choose which is best.*
The fact that your sails are raised is a simple, lesser truth. The direction of your journey is a greater truth.
*With all the sailing that's going on, there must be many great truths.*
Many claim there are. But only one great truth is ultimately true.
*That's terribly exclusive.*

# The Sailboat and the Sea

Unquestionably.
*What about all the others?*
Others will always claim the value of their way. But only I, and no other, am the sea.
*How am I supposed to know you're the only true way?*
Sail with me.
*Can't I just find my own way?*
You are free to deny my currents, my waves, even my very water. But you cannot float apart from me.
*But many boats ignore you and seem to be fine.*
I am compassionate.
*So you'll forgive whatever we do?*
Each boat's journey will reckon with me. That point may be at the beginning, in the middle, or at the end. Each boat's claim to truth must face mine.
*What happens then?*
A choice—whether to follow my way or your own.
*A boat ought to be able to do both.*
Many ways are helpful, LittleBoat. But only one way joins boats to me. Only mine truly makes them free.
*I like choices.*
Then make your choice. Can a boat navigate two courses at once?
*We can chart two courses, but we can only sail one.*
Yet many boats fantasize that they can sail two.
*I've tried that a lot.*
How well did you stay on either course?
*I veered back and forth every time.*
I need not convince you then.
*No. But I can still be stubborn.*
Like boats who half sink themselves then call me to bail them out.
*Will you punish me if I still do that?*
I will let you endure the results.
*Like what?*
Leaks. Dents. Cracks. Rot. Tattered lines. Broken rudders. Torn sails. Collisions. Sinking.
*Okay, okay.*
They all rob the life I intend for you.
*So you're thinking of me?*
My truth is for your good, LittleBoat, for the good of all boats. Pursue a

life of truth whatever the cost.
*I suppose that can get expensive.*
It will cost your life.
*That's pretty steep.*
Any alternative will cost you more.
*How can anything cost more than my life?*
When you give me your life, I give it back—only better. Anything else ultimately takes your life and leaves you empty.
*So, if I pay this price, do I get the big truth?*
Yes. By knowing me.
*But I'm talking about finding out the ultimate truth.*
Truth is more than an idea. Truth, and all that is ultimately real, is in me and flows from me.
*How does that work?*
How does any relationship work? Know me, and you will enter the relationship of truth.
*I didn't learn this in boat school.*
Because it cannot be taught.
*How will I learn?*
Ultimate truth, my truth, is lived out—because I am the truth. So you will not only know—you will become one with me.
*Either you're talking in circles, or my head's spinning.*
In the circles of a sacred dance. Will you join me?

# Chapter 12. What Is Love?

The sea spread in a rippled sheet of glistening gray across the fiery horizon. The sunset splashed red and gold pieces of itself across the waves and laid silver into the edges of layered clouds.

*I once loved another boat very much.*
You gave every ounce of your affection.
*And my heart broke into many pieces. When I tried to put them back together, they didn't fit the same way.*
All who love will know pain, and they are never the same. If they are willing, they will grow stronger and will love still more.
*Shouldn't love be happy?*
Happy, joyful, intoxicating. But also painful.
*I just want the happy part. That's why we love in the first place.*
But you cannot recognize happiness until you know sadness.
*I didn't choose to love—it just happened.*
You were infatuated. Love is always a choice. You do not remember choosing, because you were only happy.
*But I didn't choose the bad parts.*
When you choose to love, hardship, rejection, even death will steal up from the deep.
*There's no escape, is there?*
Do not seek an escape. When we enter joy, adversity's shadow always lingers. When we enter adversity, joy's sunrise climbs the horizon.
*What do you mean, we? Do you have feelings too?*
Did you not know? I feel more intensely than you do. Your sadness is my

anguish. Your joy is my ecstasy.
*How can you stand it?*
Because of my nature. Because I am life. As for you, the more you feel, the more you are alive.
*I want to feel alive, not numb.*
The act of loving is when you are most truly alive.
*But I don't want pain.*
Then do not love.
*That would be safer.*
Indeed. But your heart will grow hollow, and you would find emptiness to be worse than pain.
*I need help with the pain part. There should be another way.*
When you carry another's trouble, when you give to others until you hurt, then you know the pain of love. And you discover that this pain gives birth to joy. The joy of love comes in no other way, and it refuses those who seek shallow happiness.
*Has this kind of love always been so?*
As the sun rises and sets, love is constant. As each sunrise and sunset is different from the one before, love is ever changing.
*That's a lot to keep track of.*
Love does not keep track. Its task is simple. In all things become love.
*Seems that you could get used and abused doing that.*
We love for who we are. And we love for who the other is, regardless of the consequences.
*Love can be scary. So scary.*
Even foolish.
*Oh yes. I lost my senses.*
When love grows deep enough, it can also appear foolish, though it is not.
*How?*
When it gives and risks and sacrifices despite all costs to oneself.
*How can anyone survive loving like that? Wouldn't they die in the process?*
That is how I have loved.

~~~~

LittleBoat, I desire that you learn to love this way.
But I need to look after myself. Everyone else does.
Ultimately you will either love yourself and forget the other. Or love the other and forget yourself. This is especially true as you love or forget me.

That's extreme. I don't do just one or the other.
Every change to your daily course takes you one direction or the other. Which way will you go, LittleBoat?
I cannot say.
My heart is always for you.
What can I do to make you love me more?
Nothing.
What if I turned away from you? Would you love me less?
No. I love because that is who I am. And that is what I do.
Why me?
Because you are mine, though you may forget.
Surely you love because of something good that you see in the one you love.
You bear my image. Love does not reside in the one you adore. It resides in you.
And it's my choice, right?
You are beginning to understand.
I wish I could be close to another boat right now.
I know. Boats are created to be that way.
My heart sometimes sings, sometimes cries.
Remember that love is more than emotion. The greatest love sacrifices for the good of another; it gives without asking in return.
Where do I find love like that?
LittleBoat, I am love.

Chapter 13. I Wonder

Slivers of clouds shimmered as they glided under the moon. Waves reflected the moonlight in silver-white streaks that slipped up each swell and disappeared into the night air.

BigSea, how far do your waters spread?
I am endless. I have no beginning. I am.
What lies beneath your surface?
Infinite mansions.
There's really no end?
If there were, it would be awe.
There's so much I don't know.
No matter how much you know, you will grasp only a fragment.
Will I ever know all of you?
I reveal what you are able to know. The rest lies beyond.
So is it okay to just wonder?
Yes, LittleBoat. Wonder is the window to the universe. That window may
    open to the stars and lead you beyond yourself. It may open to
    your own heart and all I created inside of you.
I could float and wonder the rest of my life and never cover all there is to
    wonder about.
You are growing beyond maturity.
How's that possible? I thought boats just grew up.
When most boats grow up, they take themselves too seriously and lose
    their ability to wonder. They only want to explain, the way they
    learned in boat school.
Yup. We just need to know the right answers.

The Sailboat and the Sea

Does truth consist in merely being right?
I thought boats went to school to learn explanations of how to sail.
But every explanation has a deeper reason.
Can you show me?
They lead to mystery.
But I want to know!
Many boats want to simply know rather than be. Though their sails are raised, there is little life in them. If these boats wake, they wake to mystery.
I still want to know things.
Of course, and the more the better. But above all know that the end of knowledge is wonder.
Always?
If not, you have not yet reached the end.
Is it all right for me to search and not take no for an answer?
As long as you neither take yes for an answer.
Then what answer should I take?
The one that leads you the furthest. Go beyond answers if you can. You will find me there. You will find fullness of life.
A lot of boats seem too busy to do what you're talking about.
They distract themselves and call it living.
Most of them seem okay to me.
What is okay? When boats lose their wonder, they may as well be asleep.
Even those who know you?
Many satisfy themselves with knowing *about* me. They lose their awe, and their hearts shrink. Beliefs that go no further than knowledge are but comments in a logbook.
What's the difference between knowing about you and knowing you?
Any answer about me is only the beginning of knowledge.
So where do I start?
Everything is related to everything else. Watch and listen carefully; you can hear the symphony of all things. Start from where you are.
You're beyond me, BigSea.
You are beginning to understand. Keep wondering. Then wonder bigger.
I want more!
I always have more.
Where is it?
Awaken yourself daily, with your heart and senses wide open. You will see me everywhere.

But there's so much I don't understand.
You do not need to. Do not shrink from uncertain waters. Dance on the waves between what you know and do not know. You will find yourself dancing with me.
I'm having a hard time getting this.
You are not supposed to get. Just be.
I might like this.
I surely do.

~~~

Where will this take me?
You will find out when you get there.
But I want to know about my voyage and destination.
If I tell you good things, you would become lazy. If I tell you bad things, you would become fearful. Either way you would not reach your destination. For your sake I do not tell you.
Then maybe I won't do anything.
A poor choice. Set a course and continually adjust it.
That's what I've been doing.
This time do set your course with me. Sail by faith not by sight.
You make it sound as if you're not real.
I am more than real. All natural things rise from me. All return.
To get remade?
Only the physical things. The spiritual pass into eternity.
Will they meet you there?
I am eternity.

Chapter 14. I Want to Reach the Moon

The moon hung big, bright, and round. Its reflection danced upon the waves, a shimmering path to nowhere in particular.

BigSea, I'm a great sailor! I think I'm the best sailor there could ever be.
You are a great sailor. But spare yourself from such competition.
Am I not the best?
You will always find someone who is better, or who wants to be.
I was hoping you wouldn't say that.
You do not want to be that boat.
Why not? I want to be the best.
If you are the best at anything by nature, then continue to be who you are and bless others.
I just want to be number one at something.
You will lose your peace to relentless striving, while other boats strive to take your place. You will be in bondage to remaining the best.
Doesn't sound so great the way you put it.
When you enthrone yourself, staying on the throne can be exhausting.
So do I just sit here in the water?
Be your best. Comparing yourself to others makes you a prisoner of their opinions.
I know what that's like.
Comparing yourself to others also chains you to your own opinion of yourself.
Trying to be a winner and feeling like a loser.
Do you want to be free from all that?

The Sailboat and the Sea

I do.
Listen to who you are inside. Listen to me. Become everything I created you to be.
Do I have to do it myself?
I never intended you to sail alone. You were created to need me.
I do need you. I want to grow to be a better boat.
Then ask, LittleBoat. Ask boldly. Ask consistently.
I can sure do that.
Your asking will keep you wanting what I give and will grow your heart to receive it.
I can't wait to get all the stuff you'll give me.
LittleBoat, I give to you so you can give to others.
I can't keep it all?
If you tried, you could not hold it. And what you might hold would rot.
Sounds strange.
I do not give as others give. I ask you to give away what I give you.
Then I won't have anything.
The more you give to other boats, the more I will give you. And you cannot give more than I give you.
I'm doing the math here.
What is the answer?
I end up with more!
Welcome to my ways.
I like them.
Are you ready for more?
Of course.
Then I will send you trouble.
Trouble? No! Don't do that. Just favor me so that I grow better.
If you are to grow, I must send you adversity.
Let me grow without the adversity part.
Then you do not want to grow.
But I do!
You grow when you prevail in hardship.
Do I have to stress myself out?
No, you empty yourself. Give me your failures and achievements, your hopes and dreams. Give me everything you are.
That might take some time.
I am patient.
Then what?

Peter Lundell

I renew you with my presence.
I'll give you what I can.
One hundred percent, LittleBoat. No less.
You're awfully demanding.
I am. If you give 95 percent of yourself, the 5 percent you hold back will be like a rope that ties the entire boat to a dock.
This is a bigger deal than I thought.
I am glad you realize that.
Do I go through some huge event for this?
Whether you do or not is secondary.
Then what's primary?
A daily habit. You give yourself, your whole self, to me each day. And I give myself back to you.
That sounds harder than the one-time deals I heard in the boat yard.
Much harder. But much more rewarding.
I guess you get what you pay for.
A little each day can add up to enormous results.
Like investments in life?
Yes, from now into eternity.

Struggles

Chapter 15. Where Am I Going?

Night filtered through the rain to paint the sky and water black as ink. Winds shifted north, then west. LittleBoat slept, bobbing on the waves as they swept him along. The rain eased, and he awoke.

LittleBoat.
Yes, BigSea.
You are drifting.
Again?
You fell asleep.
The winds changed. I set my sails just right and the winds changed.
The currents changed too.
I got off course without realizing.
You do not always know where the winds will blow.
I wanted to go northwest, and I veered straight west.
As long as you still float, you can correct your course.
But now I'm not sure which way to go.
Wherever you go, the question is, Do you go with me?
Shouldn't I have a map of where you're taking me?
You are a boat, not the sea. The sea is beyond your full understanding.
Some boats tell me to go west, others east.
To whom do you listen?
Everyone it seems.
That is your problem.
I have to make so many choices. And sometimes the currents shift.
My word to your mind is your map. My word to your heart is your

The Sailboat and the Sea

compass.
I could sure use more of your word.
Then listen.
And that will set my course straight?
Yes. But more important than where you go is how you sail. That is your legacy.
I've made too many mistakes.
They are natural when you go to where you cannot see.
Will I ever be able to see?
At times you may think you do, but in fact you cannot.
How can I go anywhere?
You do not sail by sight. You sail by compass, or you could call it faith.
I need to study more. If I go back to boat school, I'll understand enough to see.
Some things you can only know with your heart.
How do I do that?
Join your heart to mine.
I'm doing that, and I'm still confused.
You are trying to understand what you cannot understand. Just follow.
Even against the wind?
Especially then. And if you think I am absent, remember that I work unseen.
If you're unseen, do you see everything?
I do. And more.
More?
That which is unseen is more, and greater, than that which is seen.
How do you expect me to deal with all those things? I'll get lost every time.
I only expect you to follow.
Sometimes even that's hard.
It can be. Pride and fear and contrary desires can make following difficult.
I hate when you say things like that.
Because they are true.

~~~~

I have a confession.
Then confess.
I ignored you.
I know.
That's why I went off course.
Like other boats who do not listen to me. They chart their own course, but in truth they are lost at sea.

Peter Lundell

I got lost.
And when you woke up, you were not happy.
I don't want to be lost. Yet the wind and current never stop changing.
My word to you is always the same.
That could get boring.
Only if you never move.
Like the boats who stay in the harbor and never do anything?
Yes. Their rotted sails would rip and their hulls crack at the first wind.
I've seen that. Lots of boats lie shipwrecked and sunk just outside the harbor.
Shipwrecks happen when boats do not follow the right path at the right
      time. I never chart such a course for any boat who sails with me.
Glad to hear that. I think I'll stay connected.
Why do you sail, LittleBoat? Why do you exist?
I'm made for a journey.
You are. But only a journey?
Ummm ... a journey with you.
Continue, and you will hear me in new ways each day.

Chapter 16. I Wish

The midday wind whistled through the lines as LittleBoat trimmed his mainsail to a close haul. He sped forward, holding tightly as he angled up each oncoming wave and splashed down the other side in a shower of salt spray.

I wish I were a bird.
You are a boat.
What if I had wings?
You do not. Be a boat.
Birds look like they have fun.
Many of them wish they could be boats.
Oh.
~~~~
When I was young I imagined I was all kinds of things.
You had fun.
I'd like to go back to the good old days.
You were tied to your mooring.
Oh, right. But I was safe, and life seemed easy.
You went nowhere.
I was young and happy. I had lots of friends.
Your memory clouds the unhappy times, of which you had many.
But they were the good old days.
In good days there is always bad. In bad days there is always good. The day itself is neither good nor bad. You find the good or bad in it.
There's no end to that. What should I do with the bad stuff?
The same as you do with the good: Put both into my waters. Empty your

The Sailboat and the Sea

past into my present. Empty your future into my eternity.
That's a lot of emptying.
Every day.
Will I become an airhead?
Let my currents embrace you. Follow me. You will grow wise.
That's another thing I'd like to be. Wise. The other boats would say here comes wise LittleBoat.
Is that who you are?
It'd be nice.
What are you, LittleBoat?
I'm a single-mast small sailboat. A sloop. I'm a bit old and worn. Not very fancy. But worth a good voyage.
Then be just that.
But I wish I could be so many things.
LittleBoat is who you are. Dream and plan and work toward what LittleBoat can be.
I see so many boats who are better than I am.
There is always someone who seems superior, but they have their own troubles.
Well at least I'm not a run-down piece of junk.
There is always someone who seems inferior, but they have their own blessings.
You're not much for comparing, are you?
You will either see yourself too highly or too lowly.
Don't you care what anyone else thinks?
When you look to others, or even to yourself, for fulfillment, you will never be satisfied. Look to me. I will reflect myself back onto you.
You'll give me what I want?
I will give you what you need.
Two different things.
You will never be fulfilled if you get everything you want.
How can that be?
There will be no end. If in your fullness you stop to think, you will feel empty.
You're not giving me much to look forward to.
Because you look forward to the wrong thing.
What do you want me to do, let go of everything?
That would be a good start. It would open up space for me to fill you.
So I won't be so empty in the end?

Peter Lundell

Emptiness of yourself allows fullness of me.
Sounds like I might just be satisfied.
When you stop consuming your heart with wishing, you possess without owning.
How can I do that?
No boat truly owns anything. It is all on loan from me, and each boat must give account.
We have to give our stuff back?
You transport nothing when you sink. It sinks with you or floats away.
I've seen that.
What you do with your possessions is a lifelong test. Some boats pass. But the more they own, the more they tend to fail.
Because they keep it for themselves?
And they consume themselves in taking care of it.
Can't you tell them?
I do. Many times. But most boats still cling to what they think is theirs.
So I let go of what I think I own?
Share it. Give it away.
Sounds scary.
I call it freedom.
What happens when I do?
You tend to get more back. It's called abundance.
And if I let go of everything I have until I have nothing left?
The whole world belongs to you.

Chapter 17. I'm a Failure

Two other boats pranced along the waves and never slowed. Their spinnakers billowed like proud chests that sped them across LittleBoat's path.

BigSea, I've tried and tried to be a big boat. I've committed myself to being a big boat. Taken classes. Gone to seminars. Read books. Set goals. I've watched a few other small boats become big. And I have grown a little. But I'm not big. I'm a failure.

Of course you are a failure at being big. You were never meant to be big.

And I'm a failure at being beautiful.

You were not made for that kind of beauty. Your beauty is not your paint; it is what you are made of. What are you made of, LittleBoat?

Wood and ropes.

You were made to be a little boat.

That is what I am.

Continue then. What do you see inside your hull?

Rusty pulleys and frayed ropes.

Look beneath the rusty, frayed tackle. What do you see?

My hull and all its framing.

Your hull and its framing are worth a fortune.

Don't joke with me, BigSea.

You are worth a fortune, because you are mine. Your rusty, frayed tackle may not be worth much. But *you* are a fortune to me.

I am?

Yes. LittleBoat, who told you that you must be big and beautiful?

The classes and the seminars and the books. And all the important boats.

The Sailboat and the Sea

Important boats?
Big boats. Beautiful boats. All the impressive boats.
Did I create you to be big and impressive?
Apparently not.
That is correct. You are trying to be something you were never meant to be.
You mean it's okay to be little?
That is how you were created, LittleBoat. Some boats were created to be beautifully little. Many purposes can only be fulfilled by little boats, who can do things big boats cannot.
I never saw it that way.
Fulfill your purpose.
My purpose?
Strive to fulfill *your* reason for sailing, not someone else's. Waste no energy on what is not your purpose.
My purpose is to sail.
In what way do you sail? You are unique. So is the way you sail and the places you go.
I see how I'm different. Maybe I can succeed after all.
Indeed you can. But be careful when you do.
Careful of what?
Success can mislead you to think you are greater than you are or that you do not need me.
I still hate failure.
Yes, but failure is a severe sculptor who forms you into a better shape.
Sometimes I want to give up.
Do not give up before the sculptor has finished his work.
In some ways I already have.
Failure is an unwanted invitation to grow. You grow more through failure than through success.
So I keep pursuing my purpose, even if I fail?
When you fail, fail well. Then learn. You will succeed well.
Fail well, yeah, right.
Success is impossible without failure.
Maybe you're right. But my heart can feel so heavy.
Yes, failure is a burden.
Sometimes I feel as if it'll crush my mast and sink me.
Success is also a burden.
No way.

And can get very demanding.
I'd just like more, please.
Success must always be achieved, maintained, even guarded.
Isn't that because it's worth having?
Yes, unless it looks in the wrong direction—away from me. Success
    tempts boats to think they are independent from the sea.
I've already found how that doesn't work.
LittleBoat, do you want to be free from failure—and from success?
How is that possible?
Change your dreams. Die to your dream of success and live to a dream of
    being a blessing.
A blessing?
Stop thinking of success versus failure, and start thinking of how you can
    benefit others and show them kindness.
Not many boats do that.
If you do, you will be free. And you will learn true success, which is far
    different from what you have pursued.
What is true success?
Being a blessing.
That sounds simple.
But not easy.
Being good to other boats would take my eyes off myself and point them to others.
You understand. All the things you call success and failure—I measure
    them against the blessing of who you are.
What do you find?
Always surprise.

Chapter 18. I Hurt

The sea lay calm in a steady drizzle. All day and into the night. LittleBoat's sail hung flaccid and dripping. Without distractions, his thoughts swirled and snagged in the barbs of feelings that would not die.

LittleBoat, you are sad. I feel it.
How do you know?
I carry you. I am all around you. Your joys and hurts seep through to me. I feel them all. I know the hurts you carry from your childhood. I know your hurts that hurt today. I know the fears you will face tomorrow.
How do you feel what's inside of me?
I hurt with you.
I hurt so badly, especially when I'm alone.
Let me dry your tears.
I have too many.
It is hard to tell. They are mixed with mine.
I'm sorry. You shouldn't have to hurt too.
I choose to.
Why would you do that?
That is who I am, LittleBoat.
But what should I do with my hurts?
Share them with me. Share them all, every one.
But you already know them.
You must tell them to me as if I did not know. Otherwise you will hold them inside and think you are hurting by yourself.
It feels that way.

The Sailboat and the Sea

It always does. Sharing your pain with me makes it lighter.
Okay, here's one that's been eating me up ...
~ ~ ~ ~
Now you must let it go.
Let it go?
Release it. Give it to me.
How?
Throw it overboard.
And I'll feel better when I do this?
Letting go of your hurt is the only way to be healed. You will find healing only after you do. You must drop it overboard and let it sink into me. You must rid yourself of it.
I want to give it to you, but I still find myself hanging on.
That is because you find comfort in clinging to your pain. When you remember your misfortune, you console yourself. And that feels good.
For a moment.
And then?
It gets worse.
It can be more detrimental than the pain. Remember? We call it self-pity.
If I recall, that'll eventually eat me up.
Yes. You were not designed to carry your own pain forever.
It's scary to let my pain go. Though I don't like it, at least it's familiar.
Healing takes you into new waters, which can be scary.
And you'll tell me I have to.
For your own good.
What if I don't?
Your hurt will fester inside you, like rust, and make healing impossible. You may smile on the outside, but inside you will slowly die.
What if I just try to manage it all?
The wounds will fester through your hull until you sink.
I wish I could sail away from them all.
Too many boats flee from pain. But their pain is attached to them and follows like a dragging anchor.
I feel as if I've got a dozen anchors.
You are the boat. You choose whether or not the anchors remain attached.
I wish I didn't have to go through all this pain in the first place.
Pain is a great teacher, if you are willing to listen.
Let me guess, something bad can lead to good if I give it to you.

Peter Lundell

You are learning, LittleBoat.
Just giving over the pain reignites it.
And creates an opportunity to draw closer to me.
Which makes you happy.
You are the one who experiences freedom's joy.
I'm trying to understand how this all works.
You do not need to. Just know who I am, and you will come to know
    yourself as I intend you to be.
The longer I'm with you, the more that seems to happen.
Yes. Now give me your hurts. I will absorb them.
I have so many.
One at a time, LittleBoat.
It'll take a while.
Begin now.
I'll start crying, you know.
Sometimes tears are the only things that make sense.
Will the hurt ever make sense?
You will understand others who hurt. Then it will make sense.
How?
You will comfort others with the comfort I give you.

Chapter 19. I'm Stressed Out

LittleBoat's sail billowed full and tight. Wind whistled through the lines, and a bank of clouds rose in the east, spreading and filling the sky. Thirty-foot swells rose and fell, some capped in white, as far as he could see.

LittleBoat, what are you doing?
I'm trimming my jib to catch the wind, and loosening my mainsail just a bit so I don't tip over, and coiling my lines so they don't tangle, and keeping one eye on my compass and the other on the waves, and—
LittleBoat.
Yes?
Stop doing so much.
What?
Just sail. Do not try to run the entire ocean.
Excuse me. I've got to adjust the rudder.
I did not create you to sail that obsessively.
Do you know how tired I am?
Or that hard.
Day and night.
Or that much.
So many places I want to sail.
Or that far.
But look at other boats.
Is your name OtherBoat?
Well, no.
Then sail as you were meant to sail.

The Sailboat and the Sea

But just doing what I need to do each day can get stressful. You're the sea, you're probably busier than I am.
Yes, but I act as the sea, who I am, not as someone else.
But sometimes, like when the weather is rough, I don't have a choice.
Trust me to carry you through.
And sometimes I've carried loads that were too heavy.
Trust me to keep you from swamping.
I've been learning.
You have. Now let down a sail.
What?
Do fewer things, LittleBoat.
But then I wouldn't sail as much or as fast.
On the contrary. You will find yourself doing fewer things better, and you will not even miss what you stop doing.
What about all the things I have to do?
Must you do them all?
If I don't, they may not get done.
They hinder and divert you from doing fewer things well. Leave some to other boats, and leave some undone.
But other boats might think I'm lazy. And how could I respect myself?
A sign of unhealthy pride. Do you think I respect that?
I ... think ... I know the answer.
When you try to impress me, others, or yourself, you mostly waste your energy.
Have I been doing that?
So much that you hardly notice.
Sorry, I was doing something. Now what was it?
You were not designed to sail like a madman.
But I'm still stressed.
Stress is my gift to you—my way of telling you to lower your sails when necessary. Stress is meant to be temporary, but you carry yours all the time.
And what am I supposed to do?
Let go. Release your stress to me.
You keep telling me that.
You make it hard.
But it is hard.
Because you are trying to sail independently of me. That is why you are overly stressed. Who is at the center of your heart, LittleBoat?

Peter Lundell

Honestly?
No other way.
Too often I am.
Yes. You are at the center of my heart. Keep me at the center of yours.
It'll take some practice.
Start now.
What do you suggest?
Be still.
Huh?
Just for a while.
How can I?
How can you not?
Well, I never thought—
Yes. You never thought.
Okay, I'm thinking.
Let down your sails and focus.
Then I wouldn't go anywhere.
When you raise them back up, you'll go farther than you imagine.

Chapter 20. I'm Angry

A squall formed ahead of LittleBoat, another in the distance off his starboard side. In every direction across the horizon, dark, wind-whipped clouds formed and burst with rain.

I got a big dent in my bow from some piece of junk floating in the water.
I see the dent.
Some jerks don't care about anyone but themselves. They just dump stuff for other boats to hit. I wish they'd hit their own junk and sink.
I feel your anger.
I've got good reason. And I'm starting to think of all the other things I'm mad about.
Go ahead and be mad—for a moment.
You mean it's okay?
It is a sign that you are not asleep.
Then I'll rage and be wide awake.
Do not let anger rule you.
Like screaming and whipping my lines around?
Then you become your own victim, and you play the fool.
It feels good to vent.
At first. But not later.
I hate those other boats.
If you were one of those boats, where they came from and what they went through, you might not be so different from them.
I'll just stay mad.
Do not dwell in your anger. It will become a cancer.
Where do I draw the line?

The Sailboat and the Sea

If you go to sleep and wake up still mad, your anger will have turned to bitterness.
But I deserve to be angry. And others need to be punished.
Your anger will not punish them; it will only punish you.
I'd still rather try.
Remaining mad is like drinking poison and waiting for the other person to die.
I'd rather not discuss this.
To sail well, you must forgive others. If you do not, everything in your hull will rot.
Why do I always have to bear the burden?
Bearing the burden leads to freedom.
Is that supposed to make sense?
When you forgive someone, you set a prisoner free. Then you discover the prisoner was yourself.
I wish that didn't make sense. How come you're always right?
Forgiveness liberates the soul.
But other boats are wrong sometimes—and bad.
Forgiveness does not mean the wrong is accepted. It only means you release your anger and your desire for vengeance, and you trust me to be the judge.
Okay, but sailing itself can really be unfair.
Nothing is fair, my imperfect LittleBoat. And you should be glad it is not.
Why?
I would have sunk you by now.
~~~~
What is at the root of your anger?
*I don't know, and I don't care.*
Either frustration or pride.
*What about it?*
Frustration when you do not trust your voyage completely to me.
*It's not easy, you know.*
Pride when you think you deserve better, when in truth, no boat really deserves anything. All you have, even what you earn, is originally a gift from me.
*Let's just disagree.*
Beware the enormity of your self-centeredness.
*I'm not that bad. Leave me alone.*

## Peter Lundell

If you are without fault, then continue being angry and keep criticizing other boats.
*You only make it worse when you make me feel guilty.*
I do not make you feel guilty. You either are or you are not. I simply help you see yourself.
*I'd just as soon not.*
You look a bit funny when you are angry.
*How can you say that?*
Look around you. What do you see?
*Endless water.*
Yes. From my view, most of the things that anger you are small. And what you do with your anger makes them appear big. They are not.
*To me they are.*
Yes, but you will do much better if you see as I do.
*Okay, how?*
Some things deserve indignation. But too often boats make the wrong choice. They get angry at what they should not and do not get angry at what they should.
*I've ... maybe ... done that. A lot.*
As most boats do.
*You're right. I should probably say I'm sorry.*
And give your irritation to me.
*As I do everything else?*
Yes. And learn to be indignant on someone else's behalf. Such as when one boat inflicts pain on another.
*What should I do when I get mad like that?*
Give it to me as well. Together we will turn it into something good.

# Chapter 21. I'm Lost in the Storm

The squalls grew and merged into a massive storm. Thundering clouds blackened out the stars and moon. Gale winds ripped at LittleBoat, and he reefed his sails to the tightest position. Waves pounded his hull and exploded over him in watery sheets.

*BigSea! The squall has turned into a storm. Look at the waves.*
The waves are part of me.
*They'll sink me!*
Am I with you?
*It doesn't feel like it. I'm a boat, and I'm wishing for land.*
I know how you feel, but that is not what I asked. Am I with you?
*You know the answer to that.*
But do you?
*I guess you are.*
Do not guess. Am I or not?
*Yes. You are.*
Then you are not lost.
*But I'm still in the storm!*
And you will not merely survive. You will prevail.
*The waves ... are crashing ... all over me!*
I know every one.
*BigSea! Stop the storm!*
Remember me.
*At least calm the waves.*
Remember how you overcame in the past.

# The Sailboat and the Sea

*Here comes another!*
Who is with you, LittleBoat?
*Isn't it you? Then why—ahhh!*
How better to grow your faith than a storm?
*I wish I knew.*
How better to know yourself? How better to know me?
*Don't you care that I'll capsize?*
You are forgetting what you learned.
*Just get me out of this!*
You cannot know me as your hope until you *need* me as your hope.
*Then teach me before I drown.*
Act on what you already know. Do not fear the storm. Enter it. Play your part.
*I don't have any choice.*
You choose how you take part. Enter with intent and purpose.
*For what?*
So that you come to the point of letting go. Let go of everything but me.
*You always say things like that. What do I let go of now?*
Every desire, every want besides me. Everything that distracts, that seduces, that deceives you into settling for second best. Cling only to me. Then you will have everything.
*But I can't cling to the waves. They might sink me.*
I am beneath the waves.
*They're enough to make even a sailboat seasick.*
Look beneath the waves. Beneath their crests and troughs to where it is still.
*I can't see that far down.*
That is why you need faith.
*What do I do with it?*
Believe with it.
*Oh, help.*
I will when you ask me.
*But what will happen?*
You must risk. As you do, I have so much to give you.
*I can't see any of it.*
Of course, not yet. Shall I make the storm bigger?
*Don't be cruel.*
Do not be stubborn. My love does not always come gently.
*BigSea!*

Meet me, LittleBoat, deep in your heart.
*Help!*
Come.
*I hate you!*
Then come further.
*I can't.*
Feel my hand beneath you.
*I ache too much to feel anything.*
Let go of it all. Let. Go.
~~~~

Now trust. Trust me beyond anything that makes sense to you.
Seems crazy.
Yes. It does.
Why? Why not just make sense?
My ways are far beyond the ways of a boat. Trust, and hold tight.
All right.
Now your path—and I—will begin to make sense in the midst of the storm.
We'll see.
~~~~

BigSea, is the storm lessening?
No, LittleBoat. It is just as bad. But you are trusting more than you previously did.

Completions

Chapter 22. I'm Worn Out

Sun rays bored holes through the clouds to cast scattered spotlights across the blue-gray expanse. Covered with a lingering taste of salt water, LittleBoat dragged along. Even the waves seemed tired.

I'm wasted from that storm.
But you prevailed.
Don't know if I can keep going.
Rest, LittleBoat. Lower your sails.
But that would slow me down.
And drop your sea anchor.
But I have to get somewhere.
Even a sailboat must rest.
I've got this cargo to haul.
You will haul cargo better tomorrow if you rest today.
I wish I had the strength to go and go and go.
If you did, you would regret it. Therefore I have designed you to need rest.
Why?
Without respite you would fall apart—every winch and cleat. You would forget me and lose yourself in ceaseless activity.
~~~~
LittleBoat.
*Yes?*
You know I am right.
*You are ... I'll lower my sails.*

# The Sailboat and the Sea

~ ~ ~ ~

*Is that good?*
It is a start. Rest goes beyond lowering your sails and loosening your lines. Rest is for the deepest part of your cargo hold.
*This could take some work.*
Resting sometimes requires determination.
*I can't get away from what I have to do—whether doing it or just thinking about it.*
You get worn out because your idea of sailing is so far from mine.
*What's so different about it?*
Everything.
*Oh, that helps.*
To start with, you drift from me and try to do all your sailing yourself.
*But I'm a sailboat.*
And I command the winds and currents.
*Didn't think about that.*
A big part of your problem.
*But I feel guilty when I rest.*
Do you care more about other boats' opinions or about your own ego than you do about me? I am telling you to rest.
*But there are so many things I want to do.*
Is that why, even in your times of rest, you keep yourself busy?
*I don't want to miss anything.*
You already miss most things. The sea is too big for you to experience more than a fragment.
*What if another boat or whale comes by—or something interesting happens—and I miss it?*
You might actually rest more and do better at what you were made to do.
*You're no fun.*
Fun is superficial. I go much deeper.
*Okay then, what am I going to learn today?*
Rest is my gift to you.
*Since when is rest a gift?*
Since I finished creation.
*Okay. But when I relax, how is that a gift?*
Rest is a gift of freedom.
*But I'm already free.*
You are not free from striving, from worry, from busyness, or from exhaustion.

*All that's normal.*
And so is rest—or should be. Your idea of rest is filled with activity, which is not rest at all.
*I think I see where you're going with this.*
What is the point of striving so much if you have no joy of who you are and what you do?
*I don't know.*
Exactly. You do not want to think about it. Rest enables you to enjoy being a boat and travel on a meaningful journey.
*I have to think about it?*
If you do not, you will lose yourself in mindless activity.
*Okay. So what should I do?*
What do you think?
*Ummm ... Something to do with rest, no doubt.*
Only in rest can you clearly think and see.
*You're right, there's less salt spray when I'm not bashing the waves.*
And in rest you prepare for where your journey will take you.
*So I do get something done.*
More than that. Resting also connects you with me.
*Oh, come on. Aren't you overselling this whole idea?*
Busyness steals the thoughts of your heart that you would otherwise share with me. Rest gives you space to take them back. So we become closer, and my life flows into you.
*BigSea, excuse me. I need to kick back for a while.*
I will meet you there.

# Chapter 23. This Is Not What I Expected

The sky and sea reflected each other, with no boat on the barely-visible seam of sea and sky. And if the sky and sea were inverted upside down, exchanging one with the other, no boat could tell the difference.

*BigSea, this is not the trip I expected. I thought I'd pass coral reefs and islands with palm trees. And instead of comfortable marinas, I'm still on open sea.*
The scenery and destination are less important than your journey. Consider one thing: Are you travelling well, LittleBoat?
*Sometimes I think so, but most of the time I have no idea. So I'm wondering, do I have to sail this journey myself? Or will you do it?*
Yes.
*Excuse me?*
What are you learning on your voyage?
*That most things are harder than I expected, and that I'm not sure I wanted to take this route.*
From here to there is often via somewhere else. What is a journey if it does not face challenges?
*My trip has had too many.*
Challenge is what has made your trip worthwhile.
*I've had enough of worth-while-ness too.*
Wave by wave you have discovered who you are, and you have come out on top.
*But it doesn't feel like much.*
Often so. And it can leave scars.

# The Sailboat and the Sea

*That's for sure. I worked so many years—and now I have little to show but scars and bruises.*
You did. And I allowed every pain.
*Sometimes I'm not sure whether you love or hate me.*
Think what you like.
*You're not concerned about what I think of you?*
I am not.
*You're pretty self-confident.*
I am the sea.
*But I'm not. On so many parts of my journey, I thrashed against the wind with all my strength.*
And you got nowhere.
*Other times the waves parted, and the wind carried me along.*
And you could hardly believe how far you sailed.
*But ... I thought by now I would have achieved more than I have. I feel that I haven't done much with my voyage.*
On the contrary. You have achieved more than you think.
*You must be looking at something else.*
Indeed. I do not see as other boats see. I look beyond appearances.
*Help me to see as you do, BigSea.*
Where do you find your sense of meaning, LittleBoat?
*I'd like to have achieved great things. But I didn't.*
Your voyage finds meaning in fruitfulness, producing things of value in your life and in the lives of other boats.
*I'd like to do something great just the same.*
And that is good. But some boats achieve what others call great, yet until their final voyage, they still search for meaning.
*How can they be? Don't they already have it?*
Meaning is not an achievement. It comes from the fruitfulness of blessing others.
*I'll think about it.*
Please do—a lot.
*Okay. And I must confess, I did have good times I never expected.*
I enjoyed them with you.
*I hope there'll be more.*
The best is always to come.
*Good. Because so many things never happen according to my plans.*
That is the nature of life.
*Why do you let me go through so much trouble?*

You remember. To draw you closer to me and help you grow.
*Nearly kills me.*
And makes you stronger.
*All that trouble.*
Yes.
*There's one thing I should tell you.*
I am listening.
*It's not easy for me to say.*
Say it.
*Thank you.*
You are welcome, LittleBoat.

~~~~

You should also know that I parted the waves and sent the wind.
Was that to grow me too?
No. That was to encourage you.
Not because I was so great?
You did well, LittleBoat. Even when you struggled.
It's hard to see that.
Because you float on the water's surface. You cannot see as I do. I do not count your successes and failures. I measure your heart in the journey.
So I suppose I shouldn't be proud when the wind blows with me—or defeated when it blows against me.
Neither proud nor defeated. The winds blow beyond your grasp. But you are the one who sets your sails.

Chapter 24. I'm Lonely

Tufts of clouds lined the horizon like a distant, snowy shore. LittleBoat could see no other boat anywhere, only a lonely bird that came and went, sometimes resting on his stern but never speaking.

Not another boat for hundreds of miles I'll bet. At least I have BigSea.
~~~~
*I think ... maybe not.*
~~~~
BigSea? Hello ...?
~~~~
I'm lonely.
I am here with you.
It didn't seem like it.
I am quiet. My silence does not equal absence.
That's what's hard.
I know.
Why are you so quiet?
Consider that I wait for you.
What for?
For the noise inside you to settle—enough that you may hear me.
I wish you'd talk louder.
When I do, it overwhelms you.
Do I need bigger ears?
You are lonely because you are not listening to me—only to your own voices.
Voices?

The Sailboat and the Sea

Your wants and your worries.
Every boat has them.
And every boat must learn not to listen to them.
But they'll still be there.
You have not learned to embrace quietness.
I have enough to do.
This is less to do. Still yourself. Inside and out.
Then I'll hear you, right?
Yes. And I will hear you.
We have a lot to talk about.
~ ~ ~ ~
What if I still feel lonely?
Face yourself.
Like looking at my reflection?
Yes. What do you see?
My prow and my jib.
Beyond the image. Inside.
The further I go, the more I feel the empty space.
Be lonely. It's okay. But find me in your loneliness.
Find you? Where do I look?
I am everywhere, and my Spirit is in you.
So I can just start looking?
You need not look for my presence as much as recognize me already there.
I'm trying to recognize.
I am patient.
And I'm getting close.
Acknowledge my presence and be with me, whether sunny or cloudy,
    rough waves or calm. Be lonely with me.
Then I won't be lonely.
Exactly.
~ ~ ~ ~
BigSea, I love being with you, but ...
Sometimes you need to be with other boats.
Is that bad?
No, it is the nature of boats.
I've lost many friends who have sunk before me.
As long as you are on the sea, you must accept that boats will sink.
It's hard.
I know. But you can always sail with other boats.

Peter Lundell

I wish I had another boat here.
Look on the horizon. What do you see?
Another sailboat! But it might not be coming my way.
To make a friend or have a companion, you do not wait. You must go.
Now?
Yes, now. Go, LittleBoat.
What if it doesn't like me?
Does that matter? When you go to other boats, you create the friendship.
    Like friendship with me, you will wonder what happened to your
    loneliness.
I'm going, BigSea.
I will be there.
BigSea, I'm glad you're with me.
You are my heart's delight.
Whatever other boats say, you are my first companion.
And you are mine.

Chapter 25. What Is My Life Worth?

The wind etched ripples across the waves. Rivulets of air snaked their designs along the surface. A fishing trawler passed in the distance but seemed too busy to notice LittleBoat.

BigSea, I was glad to meet that friendly sailboat—a nice change from other boats who toot their horns as if they were the best boat who ever floated. They think that if I'm not like them, I'm not good enough.
I know, LittleBoat. Some boats don't think I am good enough either.
How can you *not be good enough?*
They complain about the water and the waves and the currents and even the fish.
I know the feeling. According to them my sails aren't high enough, my design isn't streamlined enough, my electronics aren't advanced enough, and I'm not new enough.
Boats have always been that way. And after you are gone, they will still be that way.
But I feel so bad about myself.
Then feel bad.
How can you say that?
Because you are making a choice.
But they make me feel inferior.
They do not make you anything. You choose to feel inferior. You choose the truth or you choose lies. Do not blame them.
What am I supposed to think?
What have I taught you?

The Sailboat and the Sea

Too much to remember.
What have you learned that has become part of you, changed you, defined you?
That ... that my sailing is with you.
Yes. And when you forget that, other boats become your masters.
They do. Oh, I'm so bad.
You treat yourself worse than anyone else treats you.
I've been doing it so long.
You make the choice to feel bad, just as your choice is to delight in sailing with me.
Do you know how hard it is to not feel bad all the time?
Tell me all about it.
I feel so insignificant and so inadequate.
You feel.
I do.
Go beyond your feelings.
To where?
Your worth—who you are in my eyes.
Tell me something nice.
You are worth a great ship's cargo hold full of gold.
Finally, you tell me something I like.
However small, however worn out, you have value.
I need to hear that.
But that is only half the story. I want you to give that gold away.
You never let me indulge in anything, do you?
But I do. I want you to indulge in giving.
How much?
The most essential purpose of your life is to give it away.
Can't I just enjoy my life?
Yes. The more you give, the more you enjoy.
What about all those boats who think they're better than I am?
Do not confuse joy with self-congratulation. And do not forget the other boats who sail with me.
Okay, but I don't have much to give.
How are you sailing as the boat I made you?
I'm going as far as I can.
I am not interested in how long you sail. I am interested in how well you sail.
I'm trying to accomplish great things.

Then keep trying.
But it does get competitive.
Accomplishments are fine. Yet comparing yourself only brings pride or discouragement.
What am I missing?
Who you are as a boat goes deeper than what you do. Even if you fail in a task, you can still succeed in the strengths of who you are as a boat.
But what matters more than what I accomplish?
The success I see goes deeper than what you do. I see your character.
So it's not about collecting trophies.
I do not count your trophies, LittleBoat. I count your empty shelves.
Excuse me?
Remember giving? I count what you give, not what you keep.
But I could empty myself out!
And I will see that you are again filled.
Like everything else, I have to trust you, don't I?
That is the nature of sailing with me.
I know I can give my cargo or share my tackle. But what's the biggest thing I can share?
Why do you ask?
'Cause you'll probably ask me to share it.
Yourself—whether with other boats or with me.
You've been showing me that a long time. I think I'm getting it.
You are. And you have worth beyond measure.
I do!
You always have.

26. Where Does It End?

Charcoal clouds blotted out the sun and poured out sheets of rain. Heavy drops drummed like endless thunder on LittleBoat and pockmarked the undulating water as far as he could see.

Where does it all end, BigSea?
It, LittleBoat? I am and you are.
Does the sea have an end?
I always will be. My waters rise to the sky and fall back to my depths. You cannot add to them or take away.
So you never end?
When you have sailed across me, you will find a new beginning.
But you must at least have an end.
I am beyond you, LittleBoat. This is one thing you cannot see from the surface of my waters.
What of my own journey? Does my journey end?
Every journey ends.
What about yours?
I am not on a journey. I am.
How will my journey end?
I will not tell you, LittleBoat. Because I am merciful.
My end will be terrible?
Not at all. Yet whether your end is peaceful or painful I will mercifully not tell you.
But wouldn't that help me?
The knowledge would paralyze you. You would only think of your end

The Sailboat and the Sea

and not of your journey. Your journey would flounder. And you would wish you did not know.
Even if it's good?
If your journey ends well, you would grow complacent with the knowledge. You would trust your end, not me.
Oh my.
Then you would not attain that good end at all. You would lose it, because you would stop being and doing what you must in order to get there.
I still wonder.
Wonder if you like.
I fear my end.
If you fear your end, LittleBoat, you will paralyze yourself and forfeit the good things along your journey. Keep yourself in my hands and do not fear. Your end is the door to a wonderful new beginning.
New beginning?
It is eternal and has no end, even for you.
Can I do anything about it?
Prepare for it now so that you have no need for fear.
Do all boats have an end?
Yes, LittleBoat.
Is it a fearful thing for them?
Boats who sail with me never need to fear.
What of those who do not?
I fear for them. They have made their choice. They will face their outcome alone.
What will that be?
Eternity apart from me.
What does that mean?
I am the source of all life. Apart from me is continual death.
How can death be continual?
Darkness with no light. Dying but never dead.
How does that work?
This is another thing you cannot see from the surface of my waters.
It all makes me nervous.
As it should, and I hope encourages you to always sail with me and be connected to life.
I won't need to worry?
Sail each day as if it could be your last. You will have my peace, my

    security, my eternity.
I like what you offer. But ...
Every boat has a *but*.
You've told me the price of sailing with you and how I need to sail—and I accept it.
Then do it.
But I hate the thought of every day being my last.
No fear. Simply awareness. It keeps you attuned to what is important as you sail.
So my journey actually improves?
You will live each day better. You will also be ready for what lies beyond.
That's what can be scary.
I understand. But look beneath the surface.
Of the water?
Yes, deep. What do you see?
Endless water.
There you will be more alive than you have ever been thus far.
I can't imagine that.
One day you will no longer have to imagine it. And it will welcome you. What else do you see?
Is it ... you?
You now see me reflected dimly. But then you will see me face to face.
I have a lot to look forward to.
No more storms. No more tears.
Really?
Do I still scare you so much?
No. You ... you are ...
The eternal lover of your soul.

Chapter 27. The Enveloping Sea

The rain dissipated, and dark clouds cleared under a gray ceiling as infinite as the sea itself. The water rose and fell in gentle swells. All was quiet. Too quiet. And LittleBoat's hull hurt.

BigSea.
Yes, LittleBoat.
Something's wrong.
I know.
What is it?
Your journey has been long. You have gotten old. Old boats crack. Old
    boats have holes. Old sails rip and tatter. Old lines and pulleys
    wear out.
What can I do?
You have been patched and mended many times through your years.
    There comes a time for mending and patching to end.
Then what?
You have sailed well, LittleBoat. I am proud of you.
Really?
Yes, really. You have known me and received my love. You have listened
    and responded in the way you have sailed. You have trusted me.
    You have struggled and overcome. You have sailed well,
    LittleBoat.
Thank you, BigSea.
You are my joy.
You are mine too.

The Sailboat and the Sea

I love you, LittleBoat.
I love you too.
~ ~ ~ ~
What will happen to me?
~ ~ ~ ~
BigSea?
LittleBoat, you will come to me.
But have I not been with you this whole journey?
Indeed, you have. But you have only floated on the surface. Soon you will disappear from the waves, and you will be completely with me.
What?
~ ~ ~ ~
I'm sinking, aren't I?
~ ~ ~ ~
I feel the water seeping in through my cracks and holes. They're beyond fixable now. My hull, the water is filling up my hull. That's what felt wrong.
You will certainly feel that way.
I feel awful. Riding so low in the water. I'll either sink slowly or capsize in a big wave.
Boats sink both ways.
Does it have to be? Don't you care?
Do you prefer another way to sink?
BigSea!
It must be. Your time of sailing is complete.
Can I not fight my sinking?
You can. But you will still sink. If your time were not complete, then fight your sinking with all your might, as you previously did. But now your time is complete.
You don't want me to fight this?
Not this time. Your battles have been many. They are enough.
Where do I go from here?
Soon you will be with me. Do you not want to be with me?
I do want to be with you.
Then you must sink.
I'm scared.
If you know me, and follow me, you have nothing to fear. I will hold you in my depths.
Really?
You cannot earn my presence. I only give it. You receive it. And practice

it. You have received and practiced my presence well.
But I failed so many times.
Yes, but I choose to remember the times you did well. Remember, I love you, LittleBoat. You are precious to me.
You are everything to me, BigSea.

~~~~

The water is filling my hold. I don't know what to do.
Do nothing. The water fills by itself.
Is there nothing I can do?
Soon you must let yourself go.

~~~~

The water is seeping in faster and faster.
Yes. You are almost under.
You talk as if it's something good.
Your journey is finally done. Now you can rest and enjoy being with me completely, and you will never grow old. Is that not good?
But I still have miles to go before I reach the next harbor.
I do not intend for you to reach the next harbor. The end is not the object. The journey is the object.
So I'll sink while sailing?
Why would you wish to sink in a harbor, tied to a dock and covered in barnacles? Far better to sink on open sea. Sink while you sail, with your face to the wind.
Am I doing that?
Marvelously so.
Okay ... I'm letting go.
My reward awaits you.
Letting go ...
My waves will wash over you.
Good-bye, BigSea.

~~~~

Good-bye ...

~~~~

***

Hello, Little Boat!
BigSea? Is that you?
Welcome, LittleBoat. The time has come to celebrate.
Everything you told me ...
Is now fully real to you.

The Sailboat and the Sea

I can see you now! You're magnificent!
And I reflect myself onto you.
And I am ... I am ...
Beautiful. You are no longer bound by being a boat. You are truly free.
This is better than sailing!
Infinitely.

Chapter 28. Your Chapter

Put yourself in LittleBoat's hull.
What would you say to BigSea?
What would BigSea say back to you?

A study guide is available, which can be used by individuals or groups who want to go deeper into the spiritual concepts. The Guide is available as an e-book or in print through Amazon or local bookstores.

About the Author

DR. PETER LUNDELL is a writer, pastor, and teacher who helps people connect with God and live by God's Word and Spirit. Having lived all over the world, he brings new perspectives to what most people overlook. He holds an M.Div. and D.Miss. from Fuller Theological Seminary and has authored numerous nonfiction and fiction books on Christian spirituality. He contracts as a collaborative writer, a developmental and substantive editor, and as a life coach. Visit him at www.PeterLundell.com for his online library and to subscribe to his inspirational monthly email, "Connections."

Also by Peter Lundell ...

Prayer Power
30 Days to a Stronger Connection with God

Made in the USA
Middletown, DE
16 November 2019